The Two Captains

by

Friedrich Heinrich Karl, Freiherr
De La Motte-Fouque

ABOUT THE AUTHOR

Friedrich Heinrich Karl de la Motte, Baron Fouqué (12 February 1777 – 23 January 1843) was a German writer and novelist, known for his contributions to the Romantic literary movement. Born in Brandenburg an der Havel, he came from a family of French Huguenot descent, as indicated by his surname. His grandfather, Heinrich August de la Motte Fouqué, had served as a general under Frederick the Great, while his father was a Prussian army officer, a background that would influence his later works.

Fouqué is best remembered for his fantasy and romantic works, which are imbued with the ideals of heroism, honor, and the supernatural. His most famous work, Undine is a novella that blends folklore, fantasy, and the themes of love and betrayal, and is regarded as a classic of German Romantic literature. His writing often reflected the German Romantic emphasis on nature, individualism, and the mystical, positioning him as a key figure alongside other Romantic writers. Fouqué died on 23 January 1843, but his legacy as a key figure in German Romanticism endures, especially through his contributions to fantasy literature.

CONTENTS

CHAPTER I...7

CHAPTER II..11

CHAPTER III...14

CHAPTER IV...17

CHAPTER V...19

CHAPTER VI...21

CHAPTER VII..23

CHAPTER VIII..26

CHAPTER IX...28

CHAPTER X...30

CHAPTER XI...33

CHAPTER XII..35

CHAPTER XIII..37

CHAPTER XIV..39

CHAPTER XV..41

CHAPTER XVI..43

CHAPTER XVII...45

CHAPTER XVIII...47

CHAPTER XIX..49

CHAPTER I

A Mild summer evening was resting on the shores of Malaga, awakening the guitar of many a merry singer among the ships in the harbor, and in the city houses, and in many an ornamental garden villa. Emulating the voices of the birds, the melodious tones greeted the refreshing coolness, and floated like perfumed exhalations from meadow and water, over the enchanting region. Some troops of infantry who were on the shore, and who purposed to spend the night there, that they might be ready for embarkation early on the following morning, forgot amid the charms of the pleasant eventide that they ought to devote these last few hours on European soil to ease and slumber; they began to sing military songs, to drink to each other with their flasks filled to the brim with the rich wine of Xeres, toasting to the long life of the mighty Emperor Charles V., who was now besieging the pirate-nest Tunis, and to whose assistance they were about to sail. The merry soldiers were not all of one race. Only two companies consisted of Spaniards; the third was formed of pure Germans, and now and then among the various fellow-combatants the difference of manners and language had given rise to much bantering. Now, however, the fellowship of the approaching sea-voyage and of the glorious perils to be shared, as well as the refreshing feeling which the soft southern evening poured over soul and sense, united the band of comrades in perfect and undisturbed harmony. The Germans tried to speak Castilian, and the Spaniards to speak German, without its occurring to any one to make a fuss about the mistakes and confusions that happened. They mutually helped each other, thinking of nothing else but the good-will of their companions, each drawing near to his fellow by means of his own language.

Somewhat apart from the merry tumult, a young German captain, Sir Heimbert of Waldhausen, was reclining under a cork-tree, gazing earnestly up at the stars, apparently in a very different mood to the fresh, merry sociability which his comrades knew and loved in him. Presently the Spanish captain, Don Fadrique Mendez, approached him; he was a youth like the other, and was equally skilled in martial exercises, but he was generally as austere and thoughtful as Heimbert was cheerful and gentle. "Pardon, Senor," began the solemn Spaniard, "if I disturb you in your meditations. But as I have had the honor of often seeing you as a courageous warrior and faithful brother in amrs in many a hot encounter, I would gladly solicit you above all others to do me a knightly service, if it does not interfere with your own plans and projects for this night." "Dear sir," returned Heimbert courteously, "I have certainly an affair of importance to attend to before sunrise, but till midnight I am perfectly free, and ready to render you any assistance as a brother in aims." "Enough," said Fadrique, "for at midnight the tones must long have ceased with which I shall have taken farewell of the dearest being I have ever known in this my native city. But that you may be as fully acquainted with the whole affair as behoves a noble companion, listen to me attentively for a few moments.

"Some time before I left Malaga to join the army of our great emperor and to aid in spreading the glory of his arms through Italy, I was devoted, after the fashion of young knights, to the service of a beautiful girl in this city, named Lucila. She had at that time scarcely reached the period which separates childhood from ripe maidenhood, and as I—a boy only just capable of bearing arms—offered my homage with a childlike, friendly feeling, it was also received by my young mistress in a similar childlike manner. I marched at length to Italy, and as you yourself know, for we have been companions since then, I was in many a hot fight and in many an enchantingly alluring region in that luxurious land. Amid all our changes, I held unalterably within me the image of my gentle mistress, never pausing in the honorable service I had vowed to her, although I cannot conceal from you that in so doing it was rather to fulfil the word I had pledged at my departure than from any impelling and immoderately ardent feeling in my heart. When we returned to my native city from our foreign wanderings, a few weeks ago, I found my mistress married to a rich and noble knight residing here. Fiercer far than love had been was the jealousy—that almost almighty child of heaven and hell—which now spurred me on to follow Lucila's steps, from her home to the church, from thence to the house of a friend, from thence again to her home or to some noble circle of knights and ladies, and all this as unweariedly and as closely as was possible. When I had at length assured myself that no other young knight attended her, and that she devoted herself entirely to the husband chosen for her by her parents rather than desired by herself, I felt perfectly satisfied, and I should not have troubled you at this moment had not Lucila approached me the day before yesterday and whispered in my ear that I must not provoke her husband, for he was very passionate and bold; that not the slightest danger threatened her in the matter, because he loved and honored her above everything, but that his wrath would vent itself all the more furiously upon me. You can readily understand, my noble comrade, that I could not help proving my contempt of all personal danger by following Lucila more closely than ever, and singing nightly serenades beneath her flower-decked windows till the morning star began to be reflected in the sea. This very night Lucila's husband sets out at midnight for Madrid, and from that hour I will in every way avoid the street in which they live; until then, however, as soon as it is sufficiently dark to be suitable for a serenade, I will have love-romances unceasingly sang before his house. It is true I have information that not only he but Lucila's brothers are really to enter upon a quarrel with me, and it is for this reason, Senor, that I have requested you to bear me company with your good sword in this short expedition."

Heimbert seized the Spaniard's hand as a pledge of his readiness, saying as he did so, "To show you, dear sir, how gladly I will do what you desire of me, I will requite your confidence with confidence, and will relate a little incident which occurred to me in this city, and will beg you after midnight also to render me a small service. My story is short, and will not detain us longer than we must wait before the twilight has become deeper and more gloomy.

"On the day after we arrived here I amused myself with walking in the beautiful gardens with which the place abounds. I have now been long in these southern lands, but I cannot but believe that the dreams which transport me nightly back to my German home are the cause for my feeling everything here so strange and astonishing. At all events, every morning when I wake I wonder anew, as if I were only just arrived. So I was walking then, like one infatuated, among the aloe trees, which were scattered among the laurels and oleanders. Suddenly a cry sounded near me, and a slender girl, dressed in white, fled into my arms, fainting, while her companions dispersed past us in every direction. A soldier can always tolerably soon gather his senses together, and I speedily perceived a furious bull was pursuing the beautiful maiden. I threw her quickly over a thickly planted hedge, and followed her myself, upon which the beast, blind with rage, passed us by, and I have heard no more of it since, except that some young knights in an adjacent courtyard had been making a trial with it previous to a bull-fight, and that it was on this account that it had broken so furiously through the gardens.

"I was now standing quite alone, with the fainting lady in my arms, and she was so wonderfully beautiful to look at that I have never in my life felt happier than I then did, and also never sadder. At last I laid her down on the turf, and sprinkled her angelic brow, with water from a neighboring little fountain. And so she came to herself again, and when she opened her bright and lovely eyes I thought I could imagine how the glorified spirits must feel in heaven.

"She thanked me with graceful and courteous words, and called me her knight; but in my state of enchantment I could not utter a syllable, and she must have almost thought me dumb. At length my speech returned, and the prayer at once was breathed forth from my heart, that the sweet lady would often again allow me to see her in this garden; for that in a few weeks the service of the emperor would drive me into the burning land of Africa, and that until then she should vouchsafe me the happiness of beholding her. She looked at me half smiling, half sadly, and said, 'Yes.' And she has kept her word and has appeared almost daily, without our having yet spoken much to each other. For although she has been sometimes quite alone, I could never begin any other topic but that of the happiness of walking by her side. Often she has sung to me, and I have sung to her also. When I told her yesterday that our departure was so near, her heavenly eyes seemed to me suffused with tears. I must also have looked sorrowful, for she said to me, in a consoling tone, 'Oh, pious, childlike warrior! one may trust you as one trusts an angel.' After midnight, before the morning dawn breaks for your departure, I give you leave to take farewell of me in this very spot. If you could, however, find a true and discreet comrade to watch the entrance from the street, it would be well, for many a soldier may be passing at that hour through the city on his way from some farewell carouse. Providence has now sent me such a comrade, and at one o'clock I shall go joyfully to the lovely maiden."

"I only wish the service on which you require me were more rich in danger," rejoined Fadrique, "so that I might better prove to you that I am yours with life and limb. But come, noble brother, the hour for my adventure is arrived."

And wrapped in their mantles, the youths walked hastily toward the city, Fadrique carrying his beautiful guitar under his arm.

CHAPTER II

The night-smelling flowers in Lucila's window were already beginning to emit their refreshing perfume when Fadrique, leaning in the shadow of the angle of an old church opposite, began to tune his guitar. Heimbert had stationed himself not far from him, behind a pillar, his drawn sword under his mantle, and his clear blue eyes, like two watching stars, looking calmly and penetrating around. Fadrique sang:

> *"Upon a meadow green with spring,*
> *A little flower was blossoming,*
> *With petals red and snowy white;*
> *To me, a youth, my soul's delight*
> *Within that blossom lay,*
> *And I have loved my song to indite*
> *And flattering homage pay.*
>
> *"Since then a wanderer I have been,*
> *And many a bloody strife have seen;*
> *And now returned, I see*
> *The little floweret stands no more*
> *Upon the meadow as before;*
> *Transplanted by a gardener's care,*
> *And hedged by golden trellis there,*
> *It is denied to me.*
>
> *"I grudge him not his trelllsed guard,*
> *His bolts of iron, strongly barred;*
> *Yet, wandering in the cool night-air,*
> *I touch my zither's string,*
> *And as afore her beauties rare,*
> *Her wondrous graces sing,*
> *And e'en the gardener shall not dare*
> *Refuse the praise I bring."*

"That depends, Senor," said a man, stepping close, and as he thought unobserved, before Fadrique; but the latter had already been informed of his approach by a sign from his watchful friend, and he was therefore ready to answer with the greater coolness, "If you wish, Senor, to commence a suit with my guitar, she has, at all events, a tongue of steel, which has already on many occasions done her excellent service. With whom is it your pleasure to speak, with the guitar or the advocate?"

While the stranger was silent from embarrassment, two mantled figures had approached Heimbert and remained standing a few steps from him, as if to cut off Fadrique's flight in case he intended to escape. "I believe, dear sirs," said Heimbert in a courteous tone, "we are here on the same errand—namely, to prevent any intrusion upon the conference of yonder knights. At least, as far as I am concerned, you may rely upon it that any one who attempts to interfere in their affair will receive my dagger in his heart. Be of good cheer, therefore; I think we shall both do our duty." The two gentlemen bowed courteously and were silent.

The quiet self-possession with which the two soldiers carried on the whole affair was most embarrassing to their three adversaries, and they were at a loss to know how they should begin the dispute. At last Fadrique again touched the strings of his guitar, and was preparing to begin another song. This mark of contempt and apparent disregard of danger and hazard so enraged Lucila's husband (for it was he who had taken his stand by Don Fadrique) that without further delay he drew his sword from his sheath, and with a voice of suppressed rage called out, "Draw, or I shall stab you!" "Very gladly, Senor," replied Fadrique quietly; "you need not threaten me; you might as well have said so calmly." And so saying he placed his guitar carefully in a niche in the church wall, seized his sword, and, bowing gracefully to his opponent, the fight, began.

At first the two figures by Heimbert's side, who were Lucila's brothers, remained quite quiet; but when Fadrique began to get the better of their brother-in-law they appeared as if they intended to take part in the fight. Heimbert therefore made his mighty sword gleam in the moonlight, and said, "Dear sirs, you will not surely oblige me to execute that of which I previously assured you? I pray you not to compel me to do so; but if it cannot be otherwise, I must honorably keep my word, you may rely upon it." The two young men remained from that time motionless, surprised both at the decision and at the true-hearted friendliness that lay in Heimbert's words.

Meanwhile Don Fadrique, although pressing hard upon his adversary, had generously avoided wounding him, and when at last by a dexterous movement he wrested his sword from him. Lucila's husband, surprised at the unexpected advantage, and in alarm at being thus disarmed, retreated a few steps. But Fadrique threw the weapon adroitly into the air, and catching it again near the point of the blade, he said, as he gracefully presented the hilt to his opponent, "Take it, Senor, and I hope our affair of honor is now settled, as you will grant under these circumstances that I am only here to show that I fear no sword-thrust in the world. The bell of the old cathedral is now ringing twelve o'clock, and I give you my word of honor as a knight and a soldier that neither is Dona Lucila pleased with my attentions nor am I pleased with paying them; from henceforth, and were I to remain a hundred years in Malaga, I would not continue to serenade her in this spot. So proceed on your journey, and God be with you." He then once more greeted his conquered adversary with serious and solemn courtesy, and withdrew. Heimbert followed him, after having cordially shaken hands with the two youths, saying, "No, dear young sirs, do not let it ever again enter your heads to interfere in any honorable contest. Do you understand me?"

He soon overtook his companion, and walked on by his side so full of ardent expectation, and with his heart beating so joyfully and yet so painfully, that he could not utter a single word. Don Fadrique Mendez was also silent; it was not till Heimbert paused before an ornamented garden-gate, and pointed cheerfully to the pomegranate boughs richly laden with fruits which overhung it, saying, "This is the place, dear comrade," that the Spaniard appeared as if about to ask a question, but turning quickly round he merely said, "I am pledged to guard this entrance for you till dawn. You have my word of honor for it." So saying he began walking to and fro before the gate, with drawn sword, like a sentinel, and Heimbert, trembling with joy, glided within the gloomy and aromatic shrubberies.

CHAPTER III

He was not long in seeking the bright star, which he indeed felt was destined henceforth to guide the course of his whole life. The delicate form approached him not far from the entrance; weeping softly, it seemed to him, in the light of the full moon which was just rising, and yet smiling with such infinite grace, that her tears were rather like a pearly ornament than a veil of sorrow. In deep and infinite joy and sorrow the two lovers wandered silently together through the flowery groves; now and then a branch waving in the night-air would touch the guitar on the lady's arm, and it would breathe forth a slight murmur which blended with the song of the nightingale, or the delicate fingers of the girl would tremble over the strings and awaken a few scattered chords, while the shooting stars seemed as if following the tones of the instrument as they died away. Oh, truly happy was this night both to the youth and the maiden, for no rash wish or impure desire passed even fleetingly across their minds. They walked on side by side, happy that Providence had allowed them this delight, and so little desiring any other blessing that even the transitoriness of that they were now enjoying floated away into the background of their thoughts.

In the middle of the beautiful garden there was a large open lawn, ornamented with statues and surrounding a beautiful and splashing fountain. The two lovers sat down on its brink, now gazing at the waters sparkling in the moonlight, and now delighting in the contemplation of each other's beauty. The maiden touched her guitar, and Heimbert, impelled by a feeling scarcely intelligible to himself, sang the following words to it:

"There is a sweet life linked with mine,
But I cannot tell its name;
Oh, would it but to me consign
The secret of that life divine,
That so my lips in whispers sweet
And gentle songs might e'en repeat
All that my heart would fain proclaim!"

He suddenly paused, and blushed deeply, fearing he had been too bold. The lady blushed also, touched her guitar-strings with a half-abstracted air, and at last sang as if dreamily:

"By the spring where moonlight's gleams
O'er the sparkling waters pass,
Who is sitting by the youth,
Singing on the soft green grass?
Shall the maiden tell her name,
When though all unknown it be,
Her heart is glowing with her shame,
And her cheeks burn anxiously,
First, let the youthful knight be named.
'Tis he that on that glorious day
Fought in Castilla's proud array;

'Tis he the youth of sixteen years,
At Pavia, who his fortunes tried,
The Frenchman's fear, the Spaniard's pride.
Heimbert is the hero's name,
Victorious in many a fight!
And beside the valiant knight,
Sitting in the soft green grass,
Though her name her lips shall pass,
Dona Clara feels no shame "

"Oh!" said Heimbert, blushing from another cause than before, "oh, Dona Clara, that affair at Pavia was nothing but a merry and victorious tournament, and even if occasionally since then I have been engaged in a tougher contest, how have I ever merited as a reward the overwhelming bliss I am now enjoying! Now I know what your name is, and I may in future address you by it, my angelic Dona Clara, my blessed and beautiful Dona Clara! But tell me now, who has given you such a favorable report of my achievements, that I may ever regard him with grateful affection?"

"Does the noble Heimbert of Waldhausen suppose," rejoined Clara, "that the noble houses of Spain had none of their sons where he stood in the battle? You must have surely seen them fighting by your side, and must I not have heard of your glories through the lips of my own people?"

The silvery tones of a little bell sounded just then from a neighboring palace, and Clara whispered, "It is time to part. Adieu, my hero!" And she smiled on the youth through her gushing tears, and bent toward him, and he almost fancied he felt a sweet kiss breathed from her lips. When he fully recovered himself Clara had disappeared, the morning clouds were beginning to wear the rosy hue of dawn, and Heimbert, with a heaven of love's proud happiness in his heart, returned to his watchful friend at the garden gate.

CHAPTER IV

"Halt!" exclaimed Fadrique, as Heimbert appeared from the garden, holding his drawn sword toward him ready for attack. "Stop, you are mistaken, my good comrade," said the German, smiling, "it is I whom you see before you." "Do not imagine, Knight Heimbert of Waldhausen," said Fadrique, "that I mistake you. But my promise is discharged, my hour of guard has been honorably kept, and now I beg you without further delay to prepare yourself, and fight for your life until heart's blood has ceased to flow through these veins." "Good heavens!" sighed Heimbert, "I have often heard that in these southern lands there are witches, who deprive people of their senses by magic arts and incantations. But I have never experienced anything of the sort until to-day. Compose yourself, my dear good comrade, and go with me back to the shore." Fadrique laughed fiercely, and answered, "Set aside your silly delusion, and if you must have everything explained to you, word by word, in order to understand it, know then that the lady whom you came to meet in the shrubbery of this my garden is Dona Clara Mendez, my only sister. Quick, therefore, and without further preamble, draw!" "God forbid!" exclaimed the German, not touching his weapon. "You shall be my brother-in-law, Fadrique, and not my murderer, and still less will I be yours." Fadrique only shook his head indignantly, and advanced toward his comrade with measured steps for an encounter. Heimbert, however, still remained immovable, and said, "No, Fadrique, I cannot now or ever do you harm. For besides the love I bear your sister, it must certainly have been you who has spoken to her so honorably of my military expeditions in Italy." "When I did so," replied Fadrique in a fury, "I was a fool. But, dallying coward, out with your sword, or—"

Before Fadrique had finished speaking, Heimbert, burning with indignation, exclaimed, "The devil himself could not bear that!" and drawing his sword from the scabbard, the two young captains rushed fiercely and resolutely to the attack.

Different indeed was this contest to that previously fought by Fadrique with Lucila's husband. The two young soldiers well understood their weapons, and strove with each other with equal boldness, their swords flashing like rays of light as now this one now that one hurled a lightning thrust at his adversary, which was with similar speed and dexterity turned aside. Firmly they pressed the left foot, as if rooted in the ground, while the right advanced to the bold onset and then again they quickly retired to the safer attitude of defence. From the self-possession and the quiet unremitting anger with which both the combatants fought, it was evident that one of the two would find his grave under the overhanging branches of the orange-tree, which were now tinged with the red glow of morning, and this would undoubtedly have been the case had not the report of a cannon from the harbor sounded through the silence of the twilight.

The combatants paused, as if at some word of command to be obeyed by both, and listened, counting to themselves; then, as each uttered the number thirty, a second gun was heard. "It is the signal for immediate embarkation, Senor," said Don Fadrique; "we are now in the emperor's service, and all dispute ceases which is not against the foes of Charles the Fifth." "Right," replied Heimbert, "but when there is an end of Tunis and the whole war. I shall demand satisfaction for that 'dallying coward.'" "And I for that in intercourse with my sister," said Fadrique. "Certainly," rejoined the other; and, so saying, the two captains hurried down to the strand and arranged the embarkation of their troops; while the sun, rising over the sea, shone upon them both in the same vessel.

CHAPTER V

The voyagers had for some time to battle with contrary winds, and when at length they came in sight of the coasts of Barbary the darkness of evening had closed so deeply over the sea that no pilot in the little squadron ventured to ride at anchor on the shallow shore. They cruised about on the calm waters, waiting for the morning; and the soldiers, full of laudable ambition for combat, stood impatiently in crowds on the deck, straining their longing eyes to see the theatre of their future deeds.

Meanwhile the heavy firing of besiegers and besieged thundered unceasingly from the fortress of Goletta, and as the night darkened the scene with massy clouds, the flames of burning fragments became more visible, and the fiery course of the red bullets was perceptible as they crossed each other in their path, while their effects in fire and devastation were fearful to behold. It was evident that the Mussulmans had been attempting a sally, for a sharp fire of musketry burst forth suddenly amid the roaring of the cannon. The fight was approaching the trenches of the Christians, and on board the vessels none were agreed whether the besiegers were in danger or not. At length they saw that the Turks were driven back into the fortress; the Christian army pursued them, and a shout was heard from the Spanish camp as of one loud Victory! and the cry, Goletta was taken!

How the troops on board the vessels—consisting of young and courage-tried men—burned with ardor and their hearts beat at the glorious spectacle, need not be detailed to those who carry a brave heart within their own bosoms, and to all others any description would be lost. Heimbert and Fadrique stood close to each other. "I do not know," said the latter, speaking to himself, "but I feel as if to-morrow I must plant my standard upon yonder height which is now lighted up with the red glow of the bullets and burning flames in Goletta." "That is just what I feel!" said Heimbert. The two angry captains then relapsed into silence and turned indignantly away.

The longed-for morning at length dawned, the vessels approached the shore, and the landing of the troops began, while an officer was at once dispatched to the camp to announce the arrival of the reinforcements to the mighty general Alba. The soldiers were hastily ranged on the beach, they put themselves and their weapons in order, and were soon standing in battle array, ready for their great leader. Clouds of dust rose in the gray twilight, the returning officer announced the approach of the general, and as Alba signifies "morning" in the Castilian tongue, the Spaniards raised a shout of rejoicing at the coincidence, as at some favorable omen, for as the knightly train approached the first beams of the rising sun became visible.

The grave and haggard form of the general was seen mounted on a tall Andalusian charger of the deepest black. Having galloped once up and down the lines, he stopped his powerful horse in the middle, and looking along the ranks with an air of grave satisfaction, he said, "You pass muster well. That is well. I like it to be so. It is plain to see that you are tried soldiers, in spite of your youth. We will first hold a review, and then I will lead you to something more agreeable."

So saying, he dismounted, and walking toward the right wing he began to inspect one troop after another in the closest manner, with the captain of each company at his side, that he might receive from him accurate account upon the minutest particulars. Sometimes a cannon-ball from the fortress would whizz over the heads of the men; then Alba would stand still and cast a keen glance over the soldiers before him. But when he saw that not an eyelash moved, a smile of satisfaction passed over his severe pale face.

When he had inspected both divisions he again mounted his horse and once more galloped into the middle. Then, stroking his long beard, he said, "You are in good order, soldiers, and therefore you shall take your part in this glorious day, which is just dawning for our whole Christian armada. We will attack Barbarossa, soldiers. Do you not already hear the drums and fifes in the camp? Do you see him advancing yonder to meet the emperor? That side of his position is assigned to you!"

"Vivat Carolus Quintus!" resounded through the ranks. Alba beckoned the captains to him, and assigned to each his duty. He usually mingled German and Spanish troops together, in order to stimulate the courage of the combatants still higher by emulation. So it happened even now that Heimbert and Fadrique were commanded to storm the very same height, which, now gleaming with the morning light, they at once recognized as that which had shone out so fiercely and full of promise the night before.

CHAPTER VI

Thrice had Fadrique and Heimbert almost forced their way to a rampart in the fortifications, and thrice had they been repulsed with their men into the valley below by the fierce opposition of the Turks. The Mussulmans shouted after the retreating foe, clashed their weapons with the triumph of victory, and with a scornful laugh asked whether they would not come up again to give heart and brain to the scimitar and their limbs to the falling beams of wood. The two captains, gnashing their teeth with fury, arranged their ranks anew; for after three vain assaults they had to move closer together to fill the places of the slain and the mortally wounded. Meanwhile a murmur ran through the Christian army that a witch was fighting among their foes and helping them to conquer.

Duke Alba rode to the point of attack, and looked scrutinizingly at the breach they had made. "Not yet broken through the enemy here!" said he, shaking his head, "I am surprised. From two such youths, and such troops, I should have expected it." "Do you hear that? Do you hear that?" exclaimed the two captains, as they paced along their lines repeating the general's words. The soldiers shouted loudly, and demanded to be once more led against the enemy; even those who were mortally wounded shouted, with a last effort, "Forward, comrades!" The great Alba at once sprang like an arrow from his horse, wrested a partisan from the stiff hand of one of the slain, and standing in front of the two companies he cried, "I will take part in your glory. In the name of God and of the blessed Virgin, forward, my children!"

And joyfully they rushed up the hill, every heart beating with confidence, while the war-cry was raised triumphantly; some even began already to shout "Victory! victory!" and the Mussulmans paused and wavered. Suddenly, like the vision of an avenging angel, a maiden, dressed in purple garments embroidered with gold appeared in the Turkish ranks, and those who were terrified before again shouted "Allah!" calling at the same time, "Zelinda, Zelinda!" The maiden, however, drew a small box from under her arm, and opening it she breathed into it and hurled it down among the Christian troops. And forth from the fatal chest there burst a whole fire of rockets, grenades, and other fearful messengers of death. The startled soldiers paused in their assault. "Forward!" cried Alba. "Forward!" cried the two captains; but a flaming arrow just then fastened on the duke's plumed hat and hissed and crackled round his head, so that the general fell fainting down the height. Then the German and Spanish infantry fled uncontrollably from the fearful ascent. Again the storm had been repulsed. The Mussulmans shouted, and like a fatal star Zelinda's beauty shone in the midst of the flying troops.

When Alba opened his eyes, Heimbert was standing over him, with his mantle, arm, and face scorched with the fire, which he had not only just extinguished on his general's head, but by throwing himself over him he had saved him from a second body of flame rolled down the height in the same direction. The duke was thanking his youthful deliverer when some soldiers came up, looking for him, to apprise him that the Saracen power was beginning an attack on the opposite wing of the army. Without losing a word Alba threw himself on the first horse brought him and galloped away to the spot where the most threatening danger summoned him.

Fadrique stood with his glowing eye fixed on the rampart, where the brilliant form of Zelinda might be seen, with a two-edged spear, ready to be hurled, uplifted by her snow-white arm, and raising her voice, now in encouraging tones to the Mussulmans in Arabic, and again speaking scornfully to the Christians in Spanish. At last Fadrique exclaimed, "Oh, foolish being! she thinks to daunt me, and yet she places herself before me, an alluring and irresistible war-prize!"

And as if magic wings had sprung from his shoulders, he began to fly up the height with such rapidity that Alba's violent descent seemed but a lazy snail's pace. Before any one was aware, he was already on the height, and wresting spear and shield from the maiden, he had seized her in his arms and was attempting to bear her away, while Zelinda in anxious despair clung to the palisade with both her hands. Her cry for help was unavailing, partly because the Turks imagined that the magic power of the maiden was annihilated by the almost equally wondrous deed of the youth, and partly also because the faithful Heimbert, quickly perceiving his comrade's daring feat, had led both troops to a renewed attack, and now stood by his side on the height, fighting hand to hand with the defenders. This time the fury of the Mussulmans, weakened as they were by superstition and surprise, could avail nothing against the heroic advance of the Christian soldiers. The Spaniards and Germans speedily broke through the enemy, assisted by the watchful squadrons of their army. The Mohammedans fled with frightful howling, the battle with its stream of victory rolled ever on, and the banner of the holy German empire and that of the royal house of Castile waved victorious over the glorious battle-field before the walls of Tunis.

CHAPTER VII

In the confusion of the conquering and the conquered, Zelinda had wrested herself from Fadrique's arms and had fled from him with such swiftness that, however much love and desire might have given wings to his pursuit, she was soon out of sight in a spot so well known to her. All the more vehement was the fury of the excited Spaniard against the infidel foe. Wherever a little host made a fresh stand to oppose the Christians, he would hasten forward with the troops, who ranged themselves round him, resistless as he was, as round a banner of victory, while Heimbert ever remained at his side like a faithful shield, guarding off many a danger to which the youth, intoxicated with rage and success, exposed himself without consideration. The following day they heard of Barbarossa's flight from the city, and the victorious troops advanced without resistance through the gates of Tunis. Fadrique's and Heimbert's companies were always together.

Thick clouds of smoke began to curl through the streets; the soldiers were obliged to shake off the glowing and dusty flakes from their mantles and richly plumed helmets, where they often rested smouldering. "I trust the enemy in his despair has not set fire to some magazine full of powder!" exclaimed the thoughtful Heimbert; and Fadrique, allowing by a sign that he agreed with his surmise, hastened on to the spot from whence the smoke proceeded, the troops courageously pressing after him.

The sudden turn of a street brought them in view of a magnificent palace, from the beautifully ornamented windows of which the flames were emerging, looking like torches of death in their fitful glow, and lighting up the splendid building in the hour of its ruin in the grandest manner, now illuminating this and now that part of the gigantic structure, and then again relapsing into a fearful darkness of smoke and vapor.

And like some faultless statue, the ornament of the whole edifice, there stood Zelinda upon a high and giddy projection, while the tongues of flame wreathed around her from below, calling to her companions in the faith to help her in saving the wisdom of centuries which was preserved in this building. The projection on which she stood began to totter from the fervent heat raging beneath it, and a few stones gave way; Fadrique called with a voice full of anguish to the endangered lady, and scarcely had she withdrawn her foot from the spot, when the stone on which she had been standing broke away and came rattling down on the pavement. Zelinda disappeared within the burning palace, and Fadrique rushed up its marble staircase, Heimbert, his faithful companion, following him.

Their hasty steps carried them through lofty resounding halls; the architecture over their heads was a maze of high arches, and one chamber led into another almost like a labyrinth. The walls displayed on all sides magnificent shelves, in which were to be seen stored rolls of parchment, papyrus, and palm-leaf, partly inscribed with the characters of long-vanished centuries, and which were now to perish themselves. For the flames were already crackling among them and stretching their serpent-like and fiery heads from one case of treasures to another; while some Spanish soldiers, barbarous in their fury, and hoping for plunder, and finding nothing but inscribed rolls within the gorgeous building, passed from disappointment to rage, and aided the flames; the more so as they regarded the inscriptions as the work of evil magicians. Fadrique flew as in a dream through the strange half-consumed halls, ever calling Zelinda! thinking and regarding nothing but her enchanting beauty. Long did Heimbert remain at his side, until at length they both reached a cedar staircase leading to an upper story; here Fadrique paused to listen, and exclaiming, "She is speaking up there! she is speaking loud! she needs my help!" he dashed up the already burning steps. Heimbert hesitated a moment; he saw the staircase already tottering, and he thought to give a warning cry to his companion; but at the same moment the light ornamental ascent gave way and burst into flames. He could just see Fadrique clinging above to a brass grating and swinging himself up to it, but all means of following him were destroyed. Quickly recollecting himself, Heimbert lost no time in idly gazing, but hastened through the adjacent halls in search of another flight of steps which would lead him to his vanished friend.

Meanwhile Fadrique, following the enchanting voice, had reached a gallery in the midst of which, the floor having fallen in, there was a fearful abyss of flames, though the pillars on each side were still standing. Opposite to him the youth perceived the longed-for maiden, clinging with one hand to a pillar, while with the other she was threatening back some Spanish soldiers, who seemed ready at any moment to seize her, and her delicate foot was already hovering over the edge of the glowing ruins. For Fadrique to go to her was impossible; the breadth of the opening rendered even a desperate leap unavailing. Trembling lest his call might make the maiden precipitate herself into the abyss, either in terror or despairing anger, he only softly raised his voice and whispered as with a breath over the flaming gulf, "Oh,

Zelinda, Zelinda! do not give way to such frightful thoughts! Your preserver is here!" The maiden turned her queenly head, and when Fadrique saw her calm and composed demeanor, he cried to the soldiers on the other side, with all the thunder of his warrior's voice, "Back, ye insolent plunderers! Whoever advances but one step to the lady shall feel the vengeance of my arm!" They started and seemed on the point of withdrawing, when one of their number said, "The knight cannot touch us, the gulf between us is too broad for that. And as for the lady's throwing herself down—it almost looks as if the young knight were her lover, and whoever has a lover is not likely to be so hasty about throwing herself down." All laughed at this and again advanced. Zelinda tottered at the edge of the abyss. But with the courage of a lion Fadrique had torn his target from his arm, and hurling it with his right hand he flung it at the soldiers with such a sure aim that the rash leader, struck on the head, fell senseless to the ground. The rest again stood still. "Away with you!" cried Fadrique authoritatively, "or my dagger shall strike the next as surely, and then I swear I will never rest till I have found out your whole gang and appeased my rage." The dagger gleamed in the youth's hand, but yet more fearfully gleamed the fury in his eyes, and the soldiers fled. Then Zelinda bowed gratefully to her preserver, took up a roll of palm-leaves which lay at her feet, and which must have previously slipped from her hand, and then vanished hastily through a side-door of the gallery. Henceforth Fadrique sought her in vain in the burning palace.

CHAPTER VIII

The great Alba held a council with his chief officers in an open place in the middle of the conquered city, and, by means of interpreters, sent question after question to the Turkish prisoners as to the fate of the beautiful woman who had been seen animating them on the ramparts, and who was certainly the most exquisite enchantress that had ever visited the earth. Nothing very distinct was to be gained from the answers, for although the interrogated all knew of the the beautiful Zelinda as a noble lady versed in magic lore, and acknowledged by the whole people, they were utterly unable to state from whence she had come to Tunis and whither she had now fled. When at last they began to threaten the prisoners as obstinate, an old Dervish, hitherto unnoticed, pressed forward and said, with a gloomy smile, "Whoever has a desire to seek the lady may set out when he chooses; I will conceal nothing from him of what I know of her direction, and I know something. But I must first of all receive the promise that I shall not be compelled to accompany as guide. My lips otherwise will remain sealed forever, and you may do with me as you will."

He looked like one who intended to keep his word, and Alba, pleased with the firmness of the man, which harmonized well with his own mind, gave him the desired assurance, and the Dervish began his relation. He was once, he said, wandering in the almost infinite desert of Sahara, impelled perhaps by rash curiosity, perhaps by higher motives; he had lost his way there, and had at last, wearied to death, reached one of those fertile islands of that sea of sand which are called oases. Then followed, sparkling with oriental vivacity, a description of the wonderful things seen there, now filling the hearts of his hearers with sweet longing, and then again making their hair stand on end with horror, though from the strange pronunciation of the speaker and the flowing rapidity of his words the half was scarcely understood. The end of all this at length was that Zelinda dwelt on that oasis, in the midst of the pathless sand-plains of the desert, surrounded by magic horrors; and also, as the Dervish knew for certain, that she had left about half an hour ago on her way thither. The almost contemptuous words with which he concluded his narration plainly showed that he desired nothing more earnestly than to seduce some Christians to undertake a journey which must terminate inevitably in their destruction. At the same time he added a solemn oath that everything was truly as he had stated it, and he did this in a firm and grave manner, as a man who knows that he is speaking the most indubitable truth. Surprised and thoughtful, the circle of officers held their council round him.

Then Heimbert stepped forward with an air as if of request; he had just received a summons to leave the burning palace, where he had been seeking his friend, and had been appointed to the place of council because it was necessary to arrange the troops here in readiness for any possible rising in the conquered city. "What do you wish, my young hero?" said Alba, recognizing him as he appeared. "I know your smiling, blooming countenance well. You were but lately sheltering me like a protecting angel. I am so sure that you make no request but what is honorable and knightly that anything you may possibly desire is granted beforehand." "My great Duke," replied Heimbert, with cheeks glowing with pleasure, "if I may then venture to ask a favor, will you grant me permission to follow the beautiful Zelinda at once in the direction which this wonderful Dervish has pointed out?" The great general bowed in assent, and added, "So noble an adventure could not be consigned to a more noble knight!"

"I do not know that!" said an angry voice from the throng. "But well do I know that to me above all others this adventure belongs, even were it assigned as a reward for the capture of Tunis. For who was the first on the height and within the city?" "That was Don Fadrique Mendez," said Heimbert, taking the speaker by the hand and leading him before the general. "If I now for his sake must forfeit my promised reward, I must patiently submit; for he has rendered better service than I have done to the emperor and the army."

"Neither of you shall forfeit his reward," said the great Alba. "Each has permission from this moment to seek the maiden in whatever way it seems to him most advisable."

And swift as lightning the two young captains quitted the circle of officers in opposite directions.

CHAPTER IX

A sea of sand, stretching out in the distant horizon, without one object to mark its extensive surface, white and desolate in its vastness—such is the scene which proclaims the fearful desert of Sahara to the eye of the wanderer who has lost himself in these frightful regions. In this also it resembles the sea, that it casts up waves, and often a misty vapor bangs over its surface. But there is not the soft play of waves which unite all the coasts of the earth; each wave as it rolls in bringing a message from the remotest and fairest island kingdoms, and again rolling back as it were with an answer, in a sort of love-flowing dance. No; there is here only the melancholy sporting of the hot wind with the faithless dust which ever falls back again into its joyless basin, and never reaches the rest of the solid land with its happy human dwellings. There is here none of the sweet cool sea-breeze in which kindly fairies seem carrying on their graceful sport, forming blooming gardens and pillared palaces—there is only a suffocating vapor, rebelliously given back to the glowing sun from the unfruitful sands.

Hither the two youths arrived at the same time, and paused, gazing with dismay at the pathless chaos before them. Zelinda's track, which was not easily hidden or lost, had hitherto obliged them almost always to remain together, dissatisfied as Fadrique was at the circumstance, and angry as were the glances he cast at his unwelcome companion. Each had hoped to overtake Zelinda before she had reached the desert, feeling how almost impossible it would be to find her once she had entered it. That hope was now at an end; and although in answer to the inquiries they made in the Barbary villages on the frontier, they heard that a wanderer going southward in the desert and guiding his course by the stars would, according to tradition, arrive at length at a wonderfully fertile oasis, the abode of a divinely beautiful enchantress, yet everything appeared highly uncertain and dispiriting, and was rendered still more so by the avalanches of dust before the travellers' view.

The youths looked sadly at the prospect before them, and their horses snorted and started back at the horrible plain, as though it were some insidious quicksand, and even the riders themselves were seized with doubt and dismay. Suddenly they sprung from their saddles, as at some word of command, unbridled their horses, loosened their girths, and turned them loose on the desert, that they might find their way back to some happier dwelling place. Then, taking some provision from their saddle-bags, they placed it on their shoulders, and casting aside their heavy riding boots they plunged like two courageous swimmers into the trackless waste.

CHAPTER X

With no other guide than the sun by day, and by night the host of stars, the two captains soon lost sight of each other, and all the sooner, as Fadrique avoided intentionally the object of his aversion. Heimbert, on the other hand, had no thought but the attainment of his aim; and, full of joyful confidence in God's assistance, he pursued his course in a southerly direction.

Many nights and many days had passed, when one evening, as the twilight was coming on, Heimbert was standing alone in the endless desert, unable to descry a single object all round on which his eye could rest. His light flask was empty, and the evening brought with it, instead or the hoped-for coolness, a suffocating whirlwind of sand, so that the exhausted wanderer was obliged to press his burning face to the burning soil in order to escape in some measure the fatal cloud. Now and then he heard something passing him, or rustling over him as with the sound of a sweeping mantle, and he would raise himself in anxious haste; but he only saw what he had already too often seen in the daytime—the wild beasts of the wilderness roaming at liberty through the desert waste. Sometimes it was an ugly camel, then it was a long-necked and disproportioned giraffe, and then again a long-legged ostrich hastening away with its wings outspread. They all appeared to scorn him, and he had already taken his resolve to open his eyes no more, and to give himself up to his fate, without allowing these horrible and strange creatures to disturb his mind in the hour of death.

Presently it seemed to him as if he heard the hoofs and neighing of a horse, and suddenly something halted close beside him, and he thought he caught the sound of a man's voice. Half unwilling, he could not resist raising himself wearily, and he saw before him a rider in an Arab's dress mounted on a slender Arabian horse. Overcome with joy at finding himself within reach of human help, he exclaimed, "Welcome, oh, man, in this fearful solitude! If thou canst, succor me, thy fellow-man, who must otherwise perish with thirst!" Then remembering that the tones of his dear German mother tongue were not intelligible in this joyless region, he repeated the same words in the mixed dialect, generally called the Lingua Romana, universally used by heathens, Mohammedans, and Christians in those parts of the world where they have most intercourse with each other.

The Arab still remained silent, and looked as if scornfully laughing at his strange discovery. At length he replied, in the same dialect, "I was also in Barbarossa's fight; and if, Sir Knight, our overthrow bitterly enraged me then, I find no small compensation for it in the fact of seeing one of the conquerors lying so pitifully before me." "Pitifully!" exclaimed Heimbert angrily, and his wounded sense of honor giving him back for a moment all his strength, he seized his sword and stood ready for an encounter. "Oho!" laughed the Arab, "does the Christian viper still hiss so strongly? Then it only behooves me to put spurs to my horse and leave thee to perish here, thou lost creeping worm!" "Ride to the devil, thou dog of a heathen!" retorted Heimbert; "rather than entreat a crumb of thee I will die here, unless the good God sends me manna in the wilderness."

And the Arab spurred forward his swift steed and galloped away a couple of hundred paces, laughing with scorn. Then he paused, and looking round to Heimbert he trotted back and said, "Thou seemest too good, methinks, to perish here of hunger and thirst. Beware! my good sabre shall touch thee."

Heimbert, who had again stretched himself hopelessly on the burning sand, was quickly roused to his feet by these words, and seized his sword; and sudden as was the spring with which the Arab's horse flew toward him, the stout German warrior stood ready to parry the blow, and the thrust which the Arab aimed at him in the Mohammedan manner he warded off with certainty and skill.

Again and again the Arab sprung; similarly here and there, vainly hoping to give his antagonist a death-blow. At last, overcome by impatience, he approached so boldly that Heimbert, warding off the threatening weapon, had time to seize the Arab by the girdle and drag him from the fast-galloping horse. The violence of the movement threw Heimbert also on the ground, but he lay above his opponent, and holding close before his eyes a dagger, which he had dexterously drawn from his girdle, he exclaimed, "Wilt thou have mercy or death?" The Arab, trembling, cast down his eyes before the gleaming and murderous weapon, and said, "Show mercy to me, mighty warrior; I surrender to thee." Heimbert then ordered him to throw away the sabre he still held in his right hand. He did so, and both combatants rose, and again sunk down upon the sand, for the victor was far more weary than the vanquished.

The Arab's good horse meanwhile had trotted toward them, according to the habit of those noble animals, who never forsake their fallen master. It now stood behind the two men, stretching out its long slender neck affectionately toward them. "Arab," said Heimbert with exhausted voice, "take from thy horse what provision thou hast with thee and place it before me." The vanquished man humbly did as he was commanded, now just as much submitting to the will of the conqueror as he had before exhibited his animosity in anger and revenge. After a few draughts of palm-wine from the skin, Heimbert looked at the youth under a new aspect; he then partook of some fruits, drank more of the palm-wine, and at length said, "You are going to ride still farther to-night, young man?" "Yes, indeed," replied the Arab sadly; "on a distant oasis there dwells my aged father and my blooming bride. Now—even if you set me at full liberty—I must perish in the heat of this barren desert, for want of sustenance, before I can reach my lovely home."

"Is it, perhaps," asked Heimbert, "the oasis on which the mighty enchantress, Zelinda, dwells?"

"Allah protect me!" cried the Arab, clasping his hands. "Zelinda's wondrous isle offers no hospitable shelter to any but magicians. It lies far away in the scorching south, while our friendly oasis is toward the cooler west."

"I only asked in case we might be travelling companions," said Heimbert courteously. "If that cannot be, we must certainly divide the provisions; for I would not have so brave a warrior as you perish, with hunger and thirst."

So saying, the young captain began to arrange the provisions in two portions, placing the larger on his left and the smaller at his right; he then desired the Arab to take the former, and added, to his astonished companion, "See, good sir, I have either not much farther to travel or I shall perish in the desert; I feel that it will be so. Besides, I cannot carry half so much on foot as you can on horse-back."

"Knight! victorious knight!" cried the amazed Mussulman, "am I then to keep my horse?"

"It were a sin and shame indeed," said Heimbert, smiling, "to separate such a faithful steed from such a skilful rider. Ride on, in God's name, and get safely to your people."

He then helped him to mount, and the Arab was on the point of uttering a few words of gratitude, when he suddenly exclaimed, "The magic maiden!" and, swift as the wind, he flew over the dusty plain. Heimbert, however, turning round, saw close beside him in the now bright moonlight a shining figure, which he at once perceived to be Zelinda.

CHAPTER XI

The maiden looked fixedly at the young soldier, and seemed considering with what words to address him, while he, after his long search and now unexpected success, was equally at a loss. At last she said in Spanish, "Thou wonderful enigma, I have been witness of all that has passed between thee and the Arab; and these affairs confuse my head like a whirlwind. Speak, therefore, plainly, that I may know whether thou art a madman or an angel?"

"I am neither, dear lady," replied Heimbert, with his wonted friendliness. "I am only a poor wanderer, who has just been putting into practice one of the commands of his Master, Jesus Christ."

"Sit down," said Zelinda, "and tell me of thy Master; he must be himself unprecedented to have such a servant. The night is cool and still, and at my side thou hast no cause to fear the dangers of the desert."

"Lady," replied Heimbert, smiling, "I am not of a fearful nature, and when I am speaking of my dear Saviour my mind is perfectly free from all alarm."

Thus saying, they both sat down on the now cooled sand and began a wondrous conversation, while the full moon shone upon them from the deep-blue heavens above like a magic lamp.

Heimbert's words, full of divine love, truth, and simplicity sank like soft sunbeams, gently and surely, into Zelinda's, heart, driving away the mysterious magic power which dwelt there, and wrestling for the dominion of the noble territory of her soul. When morning began to dawn she said, "Thou wouldst not be called an angel last evening, but thou art truly one. For what else are angels than messengers of the Most High God?" "In that sense," rejoined Heimbert, "I am well satisfied with the name, for I certainly hope that I am the bearer of my Master's message. Yes, if he bestows on me further grace and strength, it may even be that you also may become my companion in the pious work." "It is not impossible," said Zelinda thoughtfully. "Thou must, however, come with me to my island, and there thou shalt be regaled as is befitting such an ambassador, far better than here on the desolate sand, with the miserable palm-wine that thou hast so laboriously obtained."

"Pardon me," replied Heimbert; "it is difficult to me to refuse the request of a lady, but on this occasion it cannot be otherwise. In your island many glorious things have been conjured together by your forbidden art, and many lovely forms which the good God has created have been transformed. These might dazzle my senses, and at last delude them. If you will, therefore, hear the best and purest things which I can relate to you, you must rather come out to me on this desert sand. The palm-wine and the dates of the Arab will suffice for me for many a day to come." "You would do better to come with me," said Zelinda, shaking her head with somewhat of a scornful smile. "You were certainly neither born nor brought up to be a hermit, and there is nothing on my oasis so destructive as you imagine. What is there more than shrubs and flowers and beasts gathered together from different quarters of the world, perhaps a little strangely interwoven; each, that is to say, partaking of the nature of the other, in a similar manner to that which you must have seen in our Arabian carving! A moving flower, a bird growing on a branch, a fountain gleaming with fiery sparks, a singing twig—these are truly no hateful things!" "He must avoid temptation who does not wish to be overcome by it," said Heimbert very gravely; "I am for the desert. Will it please you to come out to visit me again?" Zelinda looked down somewhat displeased. Then suddenly bending her head still lower she replied, "Yes; toward evening I shall be here again." And, turning away, she at once disappeared in the rising whirlwind of the desert.

CHAPTER XII

With the evening twilight the lovely lady returned and spent the night in converse with the pious youth, leaving him in the morning with her mind more humble, pure, and devout; and thus matters went on for many days. "Thy palm-wine and thy dates must be coming to an end," said Zelinda one evening as she presented the youth with a flask of rich wine and some costly fruits. He, however, gently put aside the gift and said, "Noble lady, I would accept your gift gladly, but I fear some of your magic arts may perhaps cleave to it. Or could you assure me to the contrary by Him whom you are now beginning to know?" Zelinda cast down her eyes in silent confusion and took her presents back. On the following evening, however, she brought similar gifts, and, smiling confidently, gave the desired assurance. Heimbert then partook of them without hesitation, and from henceforth the disciple carefully provided for the sustenance of her teacher in the wilderness.

And so, as the blessed knowledge of the truth sank more and more deeply into Zelinda's soul, so that she was often sitting till dawn before the youth, with cheeks glowing and hair dishevelled, her eyes gleaming with delight and her hands folded, unable to withdraw herself from his words, he, on his part, endeavored to make her sensible at all times that it was only Fadrique's love for her which had urged him, his friend, into this fatal desert, and that it was this same love that had thus become the means for the attainment of her highest spiritual good. She still well remembered the handsome and terrible captain who had stormed the height that he might clasp her in his arms; and she related to her friend how the same hero had afterward saved her in the burning library. Heimbert too had many pleasant things to tell of Fadrique—of his high knightly courage, of his grave and noble manners, and of his love to Zelinda, which in the night after the battle of Tunis was no longer concealed within his passionate breast, but was betrayed to the young German in a thousand unconscious expressions between sleeping and waking. Divine truth and the image of her loving hero both at once sank deep within Zelinda's heart, and struck root there with tender but indestructible power. Heimbert's presence and the almost adoring admiration with which his pupil regarded him did not disturb these feelings, for from the first moment his appearance had something in it so pure and heavenly that no thoughts of earthly love intruded. When Heimbert was alone he would often smile happily within himself, saying in his own beloved German tongue, "It is indeed delightful that I am now able consciously to do the same service for Fadrique as he did for me, unconsciously, with his angelic sister." And then he would sing some German song of Clara's grace and beauty, the sound of which rang with strange sweetness through the desert, while it happily beguiled his solitary hours.

Once when Zelinda came in the evening twilight, gracefully bearing on her beautiful head a basket of provisions for Heimbert, he smiled at her and shook his head, saying, "It is inconceivable to me, sweet maiden, why you ever give yourself the trouble of coming to me out here in the desert. You can indeed no longer find pleasure in magic arts, since the spirit of truth and love dwells within you. If you would only transform the oasis into the natural form in which the good God created it, I would go there with you, and we should have far more time for holy converse." "Sir," replied Zelinda, "you speak truly. I too have thought for some days of doing so and the matter would have been already set on foot, but a strange visitor fetters my power. The Dervish whom you saw in Tunis is with me, and as in former times we have practised many magic tricks with each other, he would like again to play the old game. He perceives the change in me, and on that account urges me all the more vehemently and dangerously."

"He must either be driven away or converted," said Heimbert, girding on his shoulder-belt more firmly, and taking up his shield from the ground. "Have the goodness, dear maiden," he continued, "to lead me to your enchanted isle."

"You avoided it so before," said the astonished Zelinda, "and it is still unchanged in its fantastic form."

"Formerly it would have been only inconsiderate curiosity to have ventured there," replied Heimbert. "You came too out here to me, and that was better for us both. But now the old enemy might lay snares for the ruin of all that the Lord has been working in you, and so it is a knightly duty to go. In God's name, then, to the work!"

And they hastened forward together, through the ever-increasing darkness of the plain, on their way to the blooming island.

CHAPTER XIII

A charming breeze began to cool the heated brows of the travellers, and the twinkling starlight revealed in the distance a grove, waving to and fro with the gentle motion of the air. Heimbert cast his eyes to the ground and said, "Go before me, sweet maiden, and guide my path to the spot where I shall find this threatening Dervish. I do not wish unnecessarily to see anything of these ensnaring enchantments."

Zelinda did as he desired, and the relation of the two was for a moment changed; the maiden had become the guide, and Heimbert, full of confidence, allowed himself to be led upon the unknown path. Branches were even now touching his cheeks, half caressingly and playfully; wonderful birds, growing out of bushes, sang joyful songs; over the velvet turf, upon which Heimbert ever kept his eyes fixed, there glided gleaming serpents of green and gold, with little golden crowns, and brilliant stones glittered on the mossy carpet. When the serpents touched the jewels, they gave forth a silvery sound. But Heimbert let the serpents creep and the gems sparkle, without troubling himself about them, intent alone on following the footsteps of his guide.

"We are there!" said she with suppressed voice; and looking up he saw a shining grotto of shells, within which he perceived a man asleep clad in golden scale-armor of the old Numidian fashion. "Is that also a phantom, there yonder in the golden scales?" inquired Heimbert, smiling; but Zelinda looked very grave and replied, "Oh, no! that is the Dervish himself, and his having put on this coat-of-mail, which has been rendered invulnerable by dragon's blood, is a proof that by his magic he has become aware of our intention." "What does that signify?" said Heimbert; "he would have to know it at last." And he began at once to call out, with a cheerful voice, "Wake up, old sir, wake up! Here is an acquaintance of yours, who has matters upon which he must speak to you."

And as the Dervish opened his large rolling eyes, everything in the magic grove began to move, the water began to dance, and the branches to intertwine in wild emulation, and at the same time the precious stones and the shells and corals emitted strange and confusing melodies.

"Roll and turn, thunder and play as you like!" exclaimed Heimbert, looking fixedly at the maze around him; "you shall not divert me from my own good path, and Almighty God has given me a good far-sounding soldier's voice which can make itself heard above all this tumult." Then turning to the Dervish he said, "It appears, old man, that you already know everything which has passed between Zelinda and me. In case, however, that it is not so, I will tell you briefly that she is already as good as a Christian, and that she is the betrothed of a noble Spanish knight. Place nothing in the way of her good intention; I advise you for your own sake. But still better for your own sake would it be if you would become a Christian yourself. Discuss the matter with me, and first bid all this mad devilish show to cease, for our religion, dear sir, speaks of far too tender and divine things to be talked of with violence or with the loud voice necessary on the field of war."

But the Dervish, burning with hatred to the Christians, had not waited to hear the knight's last words when he rushed at him with his drawn scimitar. Heimbert merely parried his thrust, saying, "Take care of yourself, sir! I have heard something of your weapons being charmed, but that will avail but little before my sword. It has been consecrated in holy places."

The Dervish sprang wildly back before the sword, but equally wildly did he spring to the other side of his adversary, who only with difficulty caught the terrible cuts of his weapon upon his shield. Like a gold-scaled dragon the Mohammedan swung himself round his antagonist with an agility which, with his long flowing white beard, was ghostly and horrible to witness. Heimbert was prepared to meet him on all sides, ever keeping a watchful eye for some opening in the scales made by the violence of his movements. At last it happened as he desired; between the arm and breast on the left side the dark garments of the Dervish became visible, and quick as lightning the German made a deadly thrust. The old man exclaimed aloud, "Allah! Allah!" and fell forward, fearful even in his fall, a senseless corpse.

"I pity him!" sighed Heimbert, leaning on his sword and looking down on his fallen foe. "He has fought nobly, and even in death he called upon his Allah, whom he looked upon as the true God. He must not lack honorable burial." He then dug a grave with the broad scimitar of his adversary, laid the corpse within it, covered it over with turf, and knelt on the spot in silent heartfelt prayer for the soul of the departed.

CHAPTER XIV

Heimbert rose from his pious duty, and his first glance fell on Zelinda, who stood smiling by his side, and his second upon the wholly changed scene around. The rocky cavern and grotto had disappeared, the distorted forms of trees and beasts, half terrible and half charming as they were, had vanished also; a gentle grassy hill sloped down on every side of the point where he stood, toward the sandy waste; springs gushed out here and there in refreshing beauty; date-trees bent over the little paths—everything, indeed, in the now opening day was full of sweet and simple peace.

"Thank God!" said Heimbert, turning to his companion, "you can now surely feel how infinitely more lovely, grand, and beautiful is everything as our dear Father has created it than it can be when transformed by the highest human art. The Heavenly Gardener has indeed permitted us, his beloved children, in his abundant mercy, to help forward his gracious works, that we may thus become happier and better; but we must take care that we change nothing to suit our own rash wilful fancies; else it is as if we were expelling ourselves a second time from Paradise." "It shall not happen again," said Zelinda humbly. "But may you in this solitary region, where we are not likely to meet with any priest of our faith, may you not bestow on me, as one born anew, the blessing of Holy Baptism?"

Heimbert, after some consideration, replied, "I hope I may do so. And if I am wrong, God will pardon me. It is surely done in the desire to bring to him so worthy a soul as soon as possible."

So they walked together, silently praying and full of smiling happiness, down to one of the pleasant springs of the oasis, and just as they reached the edge and prepared themselves for the holy work the sun rose before them as if to confirm and strengthen their purpose, and the two beaming countenances looked at each other with joy and confidence. Heimbert had not thought of the Christian name he should bestow on his disciple, but as he scooped up the water, and the desert lay around him so solemn in the rosy glow of morning, he remembered the pious hermit Antony in his Egyptian solitude, and he baptized the lovely convert, Antonia.

They spent the day in holy conversation, and Antonia showed her friend a little cave, in which she had concealed all sorts of store for her sustenance when she first dwelt on the oasis. "For," said she, "the good God is my witness that I came hither only that I might, in solitude, become better acquainted with him and his created works, without knowing at that time in the least of any magic expedients. Subsequently the Dervish came, tempting me, and the horrors of the desert joined in a fearful league with his terrible power, and then by degrees followed all that alluring spirits showed me either in dreams or awake."

Heimbert had no scruple to take with him for the journey any of the wine and fruits that were still fit for use, and Antonia assured him that by the direct way, well known to her, they would reach the fruitful shore of this waterless ocean in a few days. So with the approach of evening coolness they set out on their journey.

CHAPTER XV

The travellers had almost traversed the pathless plain when one day they saw a figure wandering in the distance, for in the desolate Sahara every object is visible to the very horizon if the whirlwind of dust does not conceal it from view. The wanderer seemed doubtful of his course, sometimes taking this, sometimes that direction, and Antonia's eastern falcon eye could discern that it was no Arab, but a man in knightly garb.

"Oh, dear sister," exclaimed Heimbert, full of anxious joy, "then it is our poor Fadrique, who is in search of thee. For pity's sake, let as hasten before he loses us, and perhaps at last his own life also, in this immeasurable waste." They strained every effort to reach the distant object, but it was now midday and the sun shone burningly upon them, Antonia could not long endure this rapid progress; added to which the fearful whirlwind soon arose, and the figure that had been scarcely visible before faded from their eyes, like some phantom of the mist in autumn.

With the rising moon they began anew to hasten forward, calling loudly upon the unfortunate wanderer, and fluttering white handkerchiefs tied to their walking-staffs, as signal flags, but it was all in vain. The object that had disappeared remained lost to view. Only a few giraffes sprang shyly past them, and the ostriches quickened their speed.

At length, as morning dawned, Antonia paused and said, "Thou canst not leave me, brother, in this solitude, and I cannot go a single step farther. God will protect the noble Fadrique. How could a father forsake such a model of knightly excellence?" "The disciple shames the teacher," replied Heimbert, his sad face brightening into a smile. "We have done our part, and we may confidently hope that God will come to the aid of our failing powers and do what is necessary." As he spoke he spread his mantle on the sand, that Antonia might rest more comfortably. Suddenly looking up, he exclaimed, "Oh, God! yonder lies a man, completely buried in the sand. Oh, that he may not be already dead!"

He immediately began to sprinkle wine, from the flask he carried, on the brow of the fainting traveller, and to chafe his temples with it. The man at last slowly opened his eyes and said, "I had hoped the morning dew would not again have fallen on me, but that unknown and unlamented I might have perished here in the desert, as must be the case in the end." So saying he closed his eyes again, like one intoxicated with sleep, but Heimbert continued his restoratives unwearyingly, and at length the refreshed wanderer half raised himself from the sand with an exclamation of astonishment.

He looked from Heimbert to his companion, and from her again at Heimbert, and suddenly exclaimed, gnashing his teeth, "Ha, was it to be thus! I was not even to be allowed to die in the dull happiness of quiet solitude! I was to be first doomed to see my rival's success and my sister's shame!" At the same time he sprang to his feet with a violent effort and rushed forward upon Heimbert with drawn sword. But Heimbert moved neither sword nor arm, and merely said, in a gentle voice, "Wearied out, as you now are, I cannot possibly fight with you; besides, I must first place this lady in security." Antonia, who had at first gazed with much emotion at the angry knight, now stepped suddenly between the two men and cried out, "Oh, Fadrique, neither misery nor anger can utterly disfigure you. But what has my noble brother done to you?" "Brother?" said Fadrique, with astonishment. "Or godfather, or confessor," interrupted Heimbert, "as you will. Only do not call her Zelinda, for her name is now Antonia; she is a Christian, and waits to be your bride." Fadrique stood fixed with surprise, but Heimbert's true-hearted words and Antonia's lovely blushes soon revealed the happy enigma to him. He sank down before the longed-for form with a sense of exquisite delight, and in the midst of the inhospitable desert the flowers of love and gratitude and confidence sent their sweetness heavenward.

The excitement of this happy surprise at last gave way to bodily fatigue. Antonia, like some drooping blossom, stretched her fair form on the again burning sand, and slumbered under the protection of her lover and her chosen brother. "Sleep also," said Heimbert softly to Fadrique; "you must have wandered about wildly and wearily, for exhaustion is pressing down your eyelids with leaden weight. I am quite fresh, and I will watch meanwhile." "Ah, Heimbert," sighed the noble Castilian, "my sister is thine, thou messenger from Heaven; that is an understood thing. But now for our affair of honor!" "Certainly," said Heimbert, very gravely, "as soon as we are again in Spain, you must give me satisfaction for that over-hasty expression. Till then, however, I beg you not to mention it. An unfinished quarrel is no good subject for conversation."

Fadrique laid himself sadly down to rest, overcome by long-resisted sleep, and Heimbert knelt down with a glad heart, thanking the good God for having given him success, and for blessing, him with a future full of joyful assurance.

CHAPTER XVI

The next day the three travellers reached the edge of the desert, and refreshed themselves for a week in an adjacent village, which, with its shady trees and green pastures, seemed like a little paradise in contrast to the joyless Sahara. Fadrique's condition especially made this rest necessary. He had never left the desert during the whole time, gaining his subsistence by fighting with wandering Arabs, and often almost exhausted by the utter want of all food and drink. At length he had become so thoroughly confused that the stars could no longer guide him, and he had been driven about, sadly and objectless, like the dust clouds of the desert.

Even now, at times, when he would fall asleep after the midday meal, and Antonia and Heimbert would watch his slumbers like two smiling angels, he would suddenly start up and gaze round him with a terrified air, and then it was not till he had refreshed himself by looking at the two friendly faces that he would sink back again into quiet repose. When questioned on the matter, after he was fully awake, he told them that in his wanderings nothing had been more terrible to him than the deluding dreams which had transported him, sometimes to his own home, sometimes to the merry camp of his comrades, and sometimes into Zelinda's presence, and then leaving him doubly helpless and miserable in the horrible solitude as the delusion vanished. It was on this account that even now waking was fearful to him, and even in sleep a vague consciousness of his past sufferings would often disturb him. "You cannot imagine it," he added. "To be suddenly transported from well-known scenes into the boundless desert! And instead of the longed-for enchanting face of my beloved, to see an ugly camel's head stretched over me inquisitively with its long neck, starting back as I rose with still more ugly timidity!"

This, with all other painful consequences of his past miseries, soon wholly vanished, from Fadrique's mind, and they cheerfully set out on their journey to Tunis. The consciousness, indeed, of his injustice to Heimbert and its unavoidable results often lay like a cloud upon the noble Spaniard's brow, but it also softened the natural proud severity of his nature, and Antonia could cling the more tenderly and closely to him with her loving heart.

Tunis, which had been before so amazed at Zelinda's magic power and enthusiastic hostility against the Christians, now witnessed Antonia's solemn baptism in a newly-consecrated edifice, and soon after the three companions took ship with a favorable wind for Malaga.

CHAPTER XVII

Beside the fountain where she had parted from Heimbert, Dona Clara was sitting one evening in deep thought. The guitar on her knees gave forth a few solitary chords, dreamily drawn from it, as it were, by her delicate hands, and at length forming themselves into a melody, while the following words dropped softly from her partly opened lips:

> *"Far away, 'fore Tunis ramparts,*
> *Where the Christian army lies,*
> *Paynim host are fiercely fighting*
> *With Spanish troops and Spain's allies.*
> *Who from bloodstained lilies there,*
> *And death's roses pale and fair —*
> *Who has borne the conquerer's prize?*
>
> *"Ask Duke Alba, ask Duke Alba,*
> *Which two knights their fame have proved,*
> *One was my own valiant brother,*
> *The other was my heart's beloved.*
> *And I thought that I should crown them,*
> *Doubly bright with glory's prize,*
> *And a widow's veil is falling*
> *Doubly o'er my weeping eyes,*
> *For the brave knights ne'er again*
> *Will be found mid living men."*

The music paused, and soft dew-drops fell from her heavenly eyes. Heimbert, who was concealed under the neighboring orange-trees, felt sympathetic tears rolling down his cheeks, and Fadrique, who had led him and Antonia there, could no longer delay the joy of meeting, but stepping forward with his two companions he presented himself before his sister, like some angelic messenger.

Such moments of extreme and sudden delight, the heavenly blessings long expected and rarely vouchsafed, are better imagined by each after his own fashion, and it is doing but an ill service to recount all that this one did and that one said. Picture it therefore to yourself, dear reader, after your own fancy, as you are certainly far better able to do, if the two loving pairs in my story have become dear to you and you have grown intimate with them. If that, however, be not the case, what is the use of wasting unnecessary words? For the benefit of those who with heart-felt pleasure could have lingered over this meeting of the sister with her brother and her lover, I will proceed with increased confidence. Although Heimbert, casting a significant look at Fadrique, was on the point of retiring as soon as Antonia had been placed under Dona Clara's protection, the noble Spaniard would not permit him. He detained his companion-in-arms with courteous and brotherly requests that he would remain till the evening repast, at which some relatives of the Mendez family joined the party, and in their presence Fadrique declared the brave Heimbert of Waldhausen to be Dona Clara's fiance, sealing the betrothal with the most solemn words, so that it might remain indissoluble, whatever might afterward occur which should seem inimical to their union. The witnesses were somewhat astonished at these strange precautionary measures, but at Fadrique's desire they unhesitatingly gave their word that all should be carried out as he wished, and they did this the more unhesitatingly as the Duke of Alba, who had just been in Malaga on some trivial business, had filled the whole city with the praises of the two young captains.

As the richest wine was now passing round the table in the tall crystal goblets, Fadrique stepped behind Heimbert's chair and whispered to him, "If it please you, Senor—the moon is just risen and is shining as bright as day—I am ready to give you satisfaction." Heimbert nodded in assent, and the two youths quitted the hall, followed by the sweet salutations of the unsuspecting ladies.

As they passed through the beautiful garden, Fadrique said, with a sigh, "We could have wandered here so happily together, but for my over-rashness!" "Yes, indeed," said Heimbert, "but so it is, and it cannot be otherwise, if we would continue to look upon each other as a soldier and a nobleman." "True!" replied Fadrique, and they hastened to reach a distant part of the garden, where the sound of their clashing swords could not reach the gay hall of betrothal they had left.

CHAPTER XVIII

Secret and inclosed, with blooming shrubs planted around, with not a sound to be heard of the merry company, nor of the animated streets of the city, with the full moon shining overhead and brightening the solemn circle with its clear brilliancy—such was the spot. The two captains unsheathed their gleaming swords and stood opposite each other, ready for the encounter. But before they began the combat a nobler feeling drew them to each other's arms; they lowered their weapons and embraced in the most fraternal manner. They then tore themselves away and the fearful contest began.

They were now no longer brothers-in-arms, no longer friends, no longer brothers-in-law, who directed their sharp steels against each other. With the most resolute boldness, but with the coolest collectedness, each fell upon his adversary, guarding his own breast at the same time. After a few hot and dangerous passes the combatants were obliged to rest, and during the pause they regarded each other with increased love, each rejoicing to find his comrade so valiant and so honorable. And then the fatal strife began anew.

With his left hand Heimbert dashed aside Fadrique's sword, which had been aimed at him with a thrust in tierce, sideward, but the keen edge had penetrated his leathern glove, and the red blood gushed out. "Hold!" cried Fadrique, and they searched for the wound, but soon perceiving that it was of no importance, and binding it up, they both began the combat with undiminished vigor.

It was not long before Heimbert's blade pierced Fadrique's right shoulder, and the German, feeling that he had wounded his opponent, now on his side called out to halt. At first Fadrique would not acknowledge to the injury, but soon the blood began to trickle down, and he was obliged to accept his friend's careful assistance. Still this wound also appeared insignificant, the noble Spaniard still felt power to wield his sword, and again the deadly contest was renewed with knightly ardor.

Presently the garden-gate clanked, and the sound of a horse's step was heard advancing through the shrubbery. Both combatants paused in their stern work and turned toward the unwelcome disturber. The next moment through the slender pines a horseman was visible whose dress and bearing proclaimed him a warrior and Fadrique, as master of the house, at once addressed him. "Senor," said he, "why you come here, intruding into a strange garden, we will inquire at another time. For the present I will only request you to leave us free from further interruption by immediately retiring, and to favor me with your name." "Retire I will not," replied the stranger, "but my name I will gladly tell you. I am the Duke of Alba." And as he spoke, by a movement of his charger a bright moonbeam fell upon his pale thin face, the dwelling-place of all that was grand and worthy and terrible. The two captains bowed low and dropped their weapons.

"I ought to know you," continued Alba, looking at them with his sparkling eyes. "Yes, truly, I know you well, you are the two young heroes at the battle of Tunis. God be praised that two such brave warriors, whom I had given up for lost, are still alive; but tell me, what is this affair of honor that has turned your good swords against each other? For I hope you will not hesitate to declare to me the cause of your knightly contest."

They complied with the great duke's behest. Both the noble youths related the whole circumstances, from the evening previous to their embarkation up to the present moment, while Alba remained between them, in silent thought, almost motionless, like some equestrian statue.

CHAPTER XIX

The Captains had already long finished their story, and the duke still remained silent and motionless, in deep reflection. At last he began to speak, and addressed them as follows:

"May God and his holy word help me, my young knights, when I say that I consider, after my best and most conscientious belief, that this affair of yours is now honorably at an end. Twice have you met each other in contest on account of those irritating words which escaped the lips of Don Fadrique Mendez and if indeed the slight wounds you have hitherto received are not sufficient compensation for the angry expression, there is still your common fight before Tunis, and the rescue in the desert afforded by Sir Heimbert of Waldhausen to Don Fadrique Mendez, after he had gained his bride for him. From all this, I consider that the Knight of Waldhausen is entitled to pardon any offence of an adversary to whom he has shown himself so well inclined. Old Roman history tells us of two captains of the great Julius Caesar who settled a dispute and cemented a hearty friendship with each other when engaged in the same bold fight, delivering each other in the midst of a Gallic army. I affirm, however, that you two have done more for each other: and therefore I declare your affair of honor to be settled, and at an end. Sheathe your swords, and embrace each other in my presence."

Obedient to the command of their general, the young knights for the present sheathed their weapons; but anxious lest the slightest possible shadow should fall on their honor they yet delayed the reconciling embrace.

The great Alba looked at them with somewhat of an indignant air, and said, "Do you then suppose, young knights, that I could wish to save the lives of two heroes at the expense of their honor? I would rather at once have struck you dead, both of you at once. But I see plainly that with such obstinate minds one must have recourse to other measures."

And, dismounting from his horse, he fastened it to a tree, and then stepped forward between the two captains with a drawn sword in his right hand, crying out, "Whoever will deny in any wise that the quarrel between Sir Heimbert of Waldhausen and Don Fadrique Mendez is honorably and gloriously settled must settle the matter at the peril of his life with the Duke of Alba; and should the present knights have any objection to raise to this, let them declare it. I stand here as champion for my own conviction."

The youths bowed submissively before the great umpire, and fell into each other's arms. The duke, however, embraced them both with hearty affection, which appeared all the more charming and refreshing as it rarely burst forth from this stern character. Then he led the reconciled friends back to their betrothed, and when these, after the first joyful surprise was over at the presence of the honored general, started back at seeing drops of blood on the garments of the youths, the duke said, smiling, "Oh, ye brides elect of soldiers, you must not shrink from such jewels of honor. Your lovers could bring you no fairer wedding gift."

The great Alba was not not be deprived of the pleasure of enacting the office of father to the two happy brides, and the festival of their union was fixed for the following day. From that time forth they lived in undisturbed and joyful concord; and though the Knight Heimbert was recalled soon afterward with his lovely consort to the bosom of his German Fatherland, he and Fadrique kept up the link between them by letters and messages; and even in after times the descendants of the lord of Waldhausen boasted of their connection with the noble house of Mendez, while the latter have ever sacredly preserved the tradition of the brave and magnanimous Heimbert.